The Kitten Story

A Mostly True Tale

By Emily Jenkins

Pictures by
Brittany Cicchese

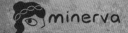
minerva

There are four people in our family. Rosie, Tulip, Daddy, and me. I am Mommy.

We decided life would be better
if we got a cat.

"Let's get an older cat," said Daddy.
"That way, we'll know its personality."

"Let's get a kitten,"
said Rosie.

"Please, let's get a
kitten," said Tulip.

Daddy shook his head. "We will get a snuggly old cat. A smart one. If we get a kitten, who knows what kind we'd be getting?"

"Kitten, kitten, kitten!"
cried the children.

Daddy shook his head again.
"We could end up with a bitey
kitten. Or a scratchy one.
An older cat is best."

The children did not agree. The conversation went on for about forty-five minutes. I'm not boring you with the whole thing.

Finally, Daddy said, "Let's have Mommy decide what we get. Mommy, I trust you to make a good decision."

So I said . . .

Kitten!

And there was rejoicing.

Except for Daddy.

I felt we should name the kitten before
we got it. Less fighting that way.

Here is a scientific method for
cat-naming, which I used:

First, I asked Tulip.

cookies! candy!
pickles!
rainbow?

Then I asked Rosie.

DEMON DESTROYER MONSTERFACE

Then I asked Daddy.

"We should be getting an older cat. Also, this naming process is not scientific at all."

I went back to Tulip.
"How about Monsterface?"

Hmmm.
How about magic bunny?

Then I went back to Rosie.
"How about Magic Bunny?"

Hmmm.
How about NIGEL?

And surprise! Tulip liked NIGEL, too.

Then I went back to Daddy.
"Oh please, anything but Nigel," he said.

I went to the animal shelter with Rosie after school.
Daddy and Tulip did not come with us. Less fighting that way.

We took a bus to a shelter we had read about.
It promised cats and dogs.

Hmmm.

There was no sign for a shelter.
It was just a house.
The neighborhood was quiet.

On the side of the house, we found a fenced-in yard. There were six dog bowls inside the fence, but no dogs.

We came back around the front.
"I don't think this is a working
animal shelter," I said.

"It's not. It's really creepy," said Rosie.
"Let's ring the bell."

"What?"

"Our kitten might be in there.
We need a kitten! It'll be worth it."

"No, Rosie. It's too creepy."

"I'm not scared. Let's ring."

A neighbor man came by. "Oh, yeah, the guy who lives there used to have an animal shelter," he said. "But he stopped doing it about four years ago. I guess he never took his website down."

Oh. Okay.
No kitten today.

Rosie and I went home on the bus. We were gloomy.

When we came home with
no kitten, Tulip cried.

The next day, I took the day off from work. Rosie and Tulip had to go to school.

"I need you to go to another shelter and bring back our kitten," Rosie told me. "I don't think I can take it if our kitten doesn't come home today."

"Get a small one!" shouted Tulip.
"Super small and very cute!"

I went far across town to visit an animal shelter that was actually open.

When I got there, I saw lots of kittens in nice cages.

They were playing ith each
other and snoozing

Some were small.
And others were
smaller.

CARL MITTENS

NINJA

He was peeking out of the carrier, so curious and bright.
He could barely even turn around in there. He wasn't small.
In fact, he was almost an older cat.
And he wasn't very cute.

He couldn't be our kitten.
But I felt sorry for him.

But there was one kitten
who wasn't in a nice cage.
He was just in a cat carrier.

"Hello," I said. "Do you need a break? Do you want to come out just for a minute to say hello?"

As soon as I picked him up, I loved him. He was snuggly. He was smart. Nothing else mattered.

This was our kitten.

I took him home on the bus and named him Blizzard. I didn't ask anybody else about the name. Less fighting that way.

Rosie loved him at first
sight. Tulip loved him, too.

There was rejoicing.

Even Daddy.

kitten, KITTEN, Kitten!

For my family —EJ

For Joe, Sherbert, and Chip —BC

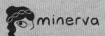minerva

An imprint of Astra Books for Young Readers,
a division of Astra Publishing House
astrapublishinghouse.com
Printed in China

ISBN: 978-1-6626-5115-1 (hc)
ISBN: 978-1-6626-5116-8 (eBook)
Library of Congress Control Number: 2022946878

First edition, 2023
10 9 8 7 6 5 4 3 2 1

Design by Jill Turney
The text is set in Limes Slab.
The illustrations were made with Procreate.